A
SAMPLER
OF
SHORT STORIES

THOMAS M. MALAFARINA

HELLBENDER BOOKS

an imprint of Sunbury Press, Inc.
Mechanicsburg, PA USA

an imprint of Sunbury Press, Inc.
Mechanicsburg, PA USA

For information about special discounts for bulk purchases, please contact Sunbury Press Orders Dept. at (855) 338-8359 or orders@sunburypress.com.

To request one of our authors for speaking engagements or book signings, please contact Sunbury Press Publicity Dept. at publicity@sunburypress.com.

FIRST HELLBENDER BOOKS EDITION: August 2021

Set in Adobe Garamond | Interior design by Crystal Devine | Cover design by Lawrence Knorr | Edited by Lawrence Knorr.

Publisher's Cataloging-in-Publication Data
Names: Malafarina, Thomas M., author.
Title: A sampler of short stories / Thomas M. Malafarina.
Description: First trade paperback edition. | Mechanicsburg, PA : Hellbender Books, 2021.
Summary: Thomas Malafarina strikes again with six spine-tingling tales of horror.
Identifiers: ISBN 978-1-62006-881-6 (softcover).
Subjects: FICTION / Horror | FICTION / Short Stories (single author).

Product of the United States of America
0 1 1 2 3 5 8 13 21 34 55

Continue the Enlightenment!

/CONTENTS/

Don't Stare, Don't Point . . . 1

Insanity . . . 9

Worms . . . 20

Bait and Switch . . . 28

Sub Sandwiches . . . 34

What Is A Man . . . 39

DON'T STARE, DON'T POINT

"It's quite stressful knowing that every time you walk out the door, someone is going to be giving you a very good look up and down, judging everything you wear."

—Emma Watson

"I'm not the judge. You know, God didn't tell me to go around judging everybody."

—Joel Osteen

"Justin Thurston Williamson, you stop that this minute. How many times do I have to tell you? It's impolite to stare and downright rude to point! You wouldn't like it if people did that to you."

That's what Justin Williamson's mother often told him back when he was a kid. However, now that he was a grown man of almost fifty, it seemed not only had he not learned his mother's lessons, but his wife Britney had taken over where his mother had left off.

"Dammit, Justin! How many times have I told you not to gawk at people and, for the love of God, don't stand there pointing at them? It's embarrassing. I don't care how odd, strange, weird, or freaky they may seem; you simply don't have the right to point them out and stare at them. I'm sure you wouldn't like it if someone stood around pointing and gaping like that at you."

"Yes, Mot . . . I mean, yes, dear," he replied, realizing he had almost said, "Yes, Mother." Whoa! That wouldn't have been a good thing by any stretch of the imagination. Because not only was his wife a lot like his long-dead mother but there were times when Justin felt as if she was his mother, reincarnated. He didn't want to begin to think about what such a concept might say about him. He decided it was probably better to keep those sorts of ideas out of his head.

"But seriously, Britt, did you see the size of that woman? She was massive. She was huge! No, she was huger than huge! She was humongous!" He started to raise his finger to point at the oversized woman again.

His wife slapped his hand down, "Justin Thurston Williamson! Don't you dare point your finger at that poor, disabled woman! She can't help it if she's disabled and has to ride around the store on that electric cart."

"Lard cart, you mean."

"Stop that! It's not funny to make a mockery of someone's disability."

"Disability? Look at the way her enormous butt hangs over both sides of the seat of that cart. It looks like two saddlebags on the back of a Harley, fat boy. It's a wonder the seat doesn't get sucked up inside her sphincter and never seen again. Look, Britt, the only disability that particular woman has is that the hole in her mouth is bigger than the one in her butt. Input exceeds output, simple math."

"But maybe she has some leg or back trouble that causes her not to be able to walk or exercise. If that's the case, she can't help but gain weight, and you shouldn't assume that she's lazy."

"It's likely a case of which came first, the chicken or the egg. Did that lady become fat because she overeats and can't exercise, or is it that she can't exercise because she overeats and is fat?"

"We don't know the answer to that. We don't know anything about the poor woman. Therefore, we have no right to judge. And we especially have no right to point and stare."

"But take a look at her husband or boyfriend or whatever the heck he is standing over there. He's skinny as a rail. What's his deal? And tell me, why is it that these enormously fat chicks always have some scrawny little man following them around like a puppy? These guys have got to be enablers, allowing those freaks to get so fat by doing everything for them. Maybe these guys are just chubby chasers and figure as long as they keep their women huge, no one else will bother with them."

"That's a terrible thing to say," Brittney scolded, looking down at herself, "I'm not exactly skin and bones, you know. I'm sure you wouldn't want people talking about me that way."

"Look, Britt. We all could stand to drop a few pounds, myself included, but these broads could stand to drop a few people, for God's sake."

He pointed at another large woman riding one of the handicapped scooters through the store. "Look at that bovine over there. You could put her in a printed tent dress and have an image of her on a banner for a sideshow, billing her as the incredible fat woman."

"I think you'd better stop this sort of talk right now, Justin. It's rude, inconsiderate, and does nothing to make you look good in anyone's eyes."

Then he pointed off in another direction, "And look at that mutant over there. He's got more tattoos and body piercings than anyone I've ever seen. He could be the star of a sideshow and billed as "The Human Pin Cushion" or "The Illustrated Man." Take a minute to look around you, Britt; the world has become an admission-free freak show, with a new oddity around every corner. No wonder you seldom see freak shows in circuses anymore. How could they possibly compete with what we see shopping here every day? So how can I help but point and stare?"

"You know Justin, someday this is all going to backfire on you, and this staring, pointing, and commenting is going to get you into big trouble."

"Trouble? Seriously? What sort of trouble could it possibly cause? It's a free country, and if some weirdo wants to parade around the same streets with normal people, then they should expect to get stared at."

"I don't know what sort of trouble could occur, but I'm telling you, Justin, no good can come of your persistent and annoying behavior."

"I think you're taking all of this a bit too seriously, Britt. It's not that big of a deal, and it's not like I do it all the time. Whoa, heads up, incoming, look over there!" He pointed toward the entrance to the store, "Now that's a real freak if I ever saw one."

"Oh my God, Justin. How can you be so insensitive? You should pity that man, not ridicule him."

"What man? Don't you mean men, as in more than one?"

Justin had been pointing at what Brittney thought at first to be a hunched-back man. But after closer examination, she realized what she saw was two men. One was normal-sized and hunched over. There was another smaller man who appeared to be attached to the front of the larger man.

"Siamese twins! Bingo! Score!" Justin shouted much louder than he should have, "Now, don't that just beat all? This store really must be a freak magnet. I mean, it's like flypaper for mutants."

"Oh, Justin! You're despicable! I've had enough of your comments. I'm leaving. You can stay here pointing and staring to your heart's content."

Brittney reached into her purse and withdrew her car keys.

"But you drove me here. How in the hell am I supposed to get home?"

"That's your problem, Justin. Maybe if you go out front in the parking lot and point at a taxicab, one will stop for you. I don't care what you do, Justin. I've had enough of you and your rude behavior for one day."

Brittany turned and walked out of the store, leaving her husband standing behind her, baffled, mouth agape.

He mumbled to himself, "I wonder what the hell's gotten into her. I mean, seriously. You make a few comments, point out a few physical flaws, and suddenly you're a bad guy? Oh well, I suppose there's nothing I can do about it now. I might as well get my shopping out of the way. Then I guess I'll call for a cab or something."

Justin turned to walk further into the store and suddenly stopped in his tracks. A crowd of strange-looking people

5

blocked his path. There had to be at least ten of them, all standing and silently staring at him. Every single one of them fit right into the category of what Justin considered to be freaks. There was a man on crutches with one leg, the empty pant leg pinned up to keep it from flapping uselessly, and a woman in a motorized wheelchair whose legs were tiny and shriveled from atrophy under her small pants. He saw the fat woman on the handicapped cart and her skinny partner. The tattooed character he thought of as the illustrated man was there as well. And at the front of the crowd stood the Siamese twins he had most recently noticed.

"Um, ah. Is there something I can do for you?" Justin asked, suddenly feeling the hairs on the back of his neck stand on end.

After several awkward moments, the tattooed man said, "You pointed at us. We saw you." Then as one, the crowd took a single step forward, feet and crutches simultaneously slapping the floor and sounding like an army on the march.

"You stared at us too," the one-legged man snarled. The crowd took another step closer.

"And you laughed at us," the fat woman said as they came even closer.

"You called us freaks," the larger Siamese twin said, followed by another step closer.

"Yeah, freaks," his smaller, conjoined brother agreed in a much higher pitch voice as they all took yet another step closer.

Justin got a good look at just how twisted and deformed the conjoined twins were. The smaller one only had a small right arm and part of a right leg. He appeared to be growing out from his brother's chest, which in essence, he was.

The larger brother said, "I wonder how you'd feel if everywhere you went, people stared and pointed at you?"

"And laughed at you and called you a freak," Some unidentified voice in the crowd shouted.

The look of the twins had so enthralled Justin; he hadn't realized the gang of oddities had somehow surrounded him.

The larger of the conjoined twins said, "But you'll know exactly how it feels very soon." That was when they all fell upon him.

///

"Justin. I'm going to the store," Brittney called. "Are you sure you don't want to come along? We have to try to get you out of the house more. I know you don't like going out in public much anymore, but maybe just this one time? It might be good for you."

She hesitated for a moment then called, "Very well; maybe next time. I won't be very long. See you soon." She was doing her best to cope with the guilt she still felt at having gotten so angry that day several months earlier when she left Justin alone in the store.

Justin didn't reply. He seldom did anymore, not since that day. He used his two twisted arms to try to struggle and lift himself into a sitting position. As difficult as this was, it had become a lot easier now that his heavy, useless, crushed legs had to be amputated. It was unbelievable how much their dead weight had slowed him down. He looked around his bedroom through his one good eye. It was the one on the side of his face that they hadn't smashed in the attack. He was also starting to see hair finally growing in random patches between the ruined areas of his pink, tender scalp. That was where the mob had torn his hair out by the roots.

He hoped someday he'd be ready to go out in public again, but he had no idea when that might be, if it ever would be at all. He knew he needed to get out and couldn't spend the rest of his life cooped up in his house. Justin knew, however, that he couldn't accept the thought that people might be staring and pointing at him.

INSANITY

"In individuals, insanity is rare; but in groups, parties, nations and epochs, it is the rule." —FRIEDRICH NIETZSCHE

"Insanity—a perfectly rational adjustment to an insane world." —R. D. LAING

"Insanity is the final surrender." —MARTA CAMINERO-SANTANGELO

"I guess if everybody went crazy together, nobody would notice." —CORMAC MCCARTHY

/ ONE /

The previous months seemed endless with day-after-dreary-day dark clouds, ceaseless rain, and damp chill air. It had been one of the gloomiest springs and summers in recorded local history with hardly a single full day of sunshine over the past six months. But now, finally, the sun had managed to slice its way through the gloom. If even if only for a brief time, it had succeeded in illuminating the city park over this much-needed lunch hour with all its radiant glory.

Tad Dresden sat on the park bench, eyes closed with his face pointed directly upward into the brightness, absorbing every luminescent ray the sun could provide. He had chosen to sneak out a few minutes early and beat the crowd of what likely would be several hundred people once the clock struck noon. He had followed the weather forecast and knew this brief teaser of sunshine would be short-lived. The forecast said the rain would resume by 2 pm, with no end in sight. He might even extend his lunch hour a bit past one to enjoy the sun while it lasted. After all, his boss was on vacation in Florida and would have no idea if he did.

He couldn't blame his boss for skipping town for a while. Tad wondered how much more of this constant rain he could take as he had so many times during the past months. He and many of his coworkers had questioned at what point the never-ending gloom would drive them all crazy.

"You might not want to get too used to that sunshine, my friend. From what the weatherman says, it ain't gonna last much longer," an elderly-sounding voice said from nearby.

Not opening his eyes or changing his position, Tad replied, "That might be true, but I still plan on soaking up as much Vitamin D as possible, thank you very much."

"Nobody can blame you for that," the voice said with a chuckle, and Tad noticed the sound of the man's footfalls getting further away. He hoped he hadn't come across as rude or unfriendly. After all, the man had only been trying to strike up a conversation. But this was the first sunshine Tad had felt in weeks, and he couldn't seem to pull himself away from it.

A few minutes later, he heard the sound of shuffling along the concrete path approaching him. At first, he thought it might be the previous stranger returning, perhaps to make another attempt at conversation. Tad hoped not, as all he wanted was to soak in more of this incredible sunshine. Then he thought, hadn't that stranger's footsteps sounded normal, like regular footfall? These didn't sound like normal footsteps at all, but we're more like an erratic dragging along the walkway. He suddenly realized just how vulnerable he was sitting there; face pointed skyward with his eyes closed. Any mugger could walk up to him with a club, bash his skull to a pulp before he even had time to react. Even in this active part in a relatively safe part of town, there were no guarantees.

Tad heard a strange monotone voice coming from directly in front of him murmuring in some unknown language he couldn't begin to identify, "Mula roo. Wallama tang. Foona taloon."

He cautiously opened his eyes to see a strange man standing in front of him, not more than three feet away. He appeared to be in his mid-thirties with a receding black hairline already showing signs of gray. He wore dark brown dress pants, matching socks and shoes, a white shirt with a tan tie. At first glance, the man would have looked like any one of a dozen office workers out for a lunchtime stroll. That was except for the crimson stain on the front of his shirt and tie. Not to mention the bloody box cutter he held tightly in his right hand.

"Fargar muffta varnoff palantarf," the man jabbered incoherently. That was when Tad noticed the man's eyes for the first time. Somehow those eyes had simultaneously managed to alternate between dead and void of all emotion to the wild eyes of a vicious, crazed animal.

"Look, buddy," Tad said with a quivering voice, "I . . . I don't want any trouble." Tad wasn't a big man, only about 5-6 and 135 pounds soaking wet. He knew nothing about self-defense and had never been in a single fight in his entire life, but he sensed the threat level was about to go nuclear. Tad slowly brought his cellphone around, prepared to call 911 if the need arose. He thought a whole lot of good that would do him if this weirdo decided to go ballistic. If the wacko was so inclined, he could slice Tad to ribbons long before any cops arrived.

To Tad's surprise, the man didn't attack, however, nor did he respond in any way to the attempts Tad made to calm him. It was like he hadn't heard a single word Tad had spoken. He just stood staring wide-eyed as a broad Jack-O-Lantern grin began to spread across his face. Tad ventured a glance down at his smartphone and pressed the telephone icon.

Then to Tad's horror, the man lifted the blood-splattered box cutter and placed the tip of its razor edge against his forehead at the place where flesh met his thinning hairline. Tad grimaced in stunned disbelief as the man sunk the blade a quarter of an inch into his forehead, not so much as flinching from what had to be an incredible level of pain. Tad felt the phone fall from his grip and clatter to the park bench, but he was too shocked by what he saw to retrieve it.

Slowly the man dug the blade across his forehead, then down the left side of his face as blood streamed over his now bulging eyes. Still, the man smiled that ridiculous

Cheshire Cat grin, blood tricking into his lips. Somewhere in the back of Tad's mind, a voice was screaming at him to find his phone, call 911 and get away from the maniac as quickly as possible. Yet he sat staring, transfixed.

The man's lips were in constant silent motion. Tad was sure the stranger must still be murmuring those bizarre, unintelligible words. When the blade had cut its way to just below the man's chin, he repeated the process on the right side of his face, completing the macabre bloody circle.

The stranger released the box cutter allowing it to clatter to the pavement. He began gradually increasing the volume of his voice as he lifted both of his hands toward his forehead. Tad's stomach churned with disgust as the man dug his fingernails deep into the groove he had sliced into his forehead.

"Mongoda denolla avatar yulunda!" The man screamed as he began peeling down the flesh from his face, pulling it off in one piece like some hideous latex mask. Tad heard ripping sounds as flesh separated from musculature. As he looked on in disbelief, he saw the man's crimson under-face revealed. The stranger tossed the skin mask aside, shouting, "Dura haarmazolla! Dura haarmazolla!"

Before Tad could react, if he was still even capable of responding, the now faceless madman turned and ran screaming across the nearby grassy park for a few dozen yards before collapsing to the ground, lying face down. His body twitched and convulsed for a few moments, then became motionless. Tad had never seen a man die before and most certainly not in such a revolting self-inflicted manner. He sat staring in awe at the unmoving mass of tattered humanity lying on the ground before him.

A series of tremors began somewhere deep inside Tad's stomach and quickly spread throughout his body in ever-increasing intensity, like ripples of water radiating from the epicenter of a rock dropped in a pond. He heard someone screaming a series of unintelligible gibberish words, and as he felt a slow stream of drool trickling down his chin, he realized the voice he heard was his own.

/ TWO /

About thirty feet across the park, an attractive, professionally dressed woman named Emma Larson stopped in her tracks, staring in confusion at the man on the park bench. At first glance, he appeared to be a typical office worker dressed in the shirtsleeves and tie uniform she had seen thousands of times. But there was nothing ordinary about the way he was acting. The man, mumbling to himself, quaked from head to toe as if in convulsion. Emma had encountered more than her share of crazy homeless street people in her life, but this character didn't seem to fit that profile.

She saw him staring off to the left, and following his gaze, she saw another man lying in a heap on the nearby grass. That man was motionless, and at first, he appeared to have a red cloth draped over his face. Then Emma saw the crimson stains on his shirt and realized the man was dead. What she thought to be a red cloth was no cloth at all but the man's face. And what had happened to him? He looked as though someone had beaten him to a pulp. Perhaps it had been that shivering man sitting on the park bench. Maybe he had hit the other man or shot him in the face. Could that be? Emma quickly took cover behind a large oak tree and fished her cellphone from her purse with trembling fingers.

Emma quickly keyed 911, desperate to hear the operator's voice. She peeked around the tree, venturing a look back at the man on the park bench. To her shock, he was now staring back at her. He raised his right arm, pointed directly at Emma, and shouted, "Garnog mon dragoob balute!"

She remembered her phone. Why hadn't the 911 operator responded? She looked down and saw she had forgotten to press the call icon. She pushed it quickly as she looked back at the man on the bench again. He now was standing, and upon seeing her, he began running toward her rapidly driven by nothing short of madness. Emma had never seen another human running so fast and knew she could never outrun him. But she quickly learned he had no intention of chasing her; it was the tree she hid behind which caught his interest.

"Aronda mogolup grontach," the man screamed at the top of his lungs as he slammed himself face-first into the trunk of the tree. The man backed away and repeated the process, each time ramming his face harder and harder until it looked like a sagging pile of raw hamburger meat. After a few final attempts, the man slid down the tree, lying unconscious or dead at its base.

Emma dropped her phone to the grass and cautiously walked around to the front of the tree. A ruby red accumulation of blood, hair, and bits of flesh coated its bark. Looking down at the man, she saw his skull had cracked open and gray matter slowly dribbled out onto the grass.

In the distance, she heard a faint voice saying, "911 operator. What is the nature of your emergency?"

Emma didn't respond. She didn't hear. She couldn't hear. She was too overwhelmed by the sounds coming from her mouth. They were words she had never heard before, if they were words at all. At first, they seemed like nonsensical gibberish until they weren't.

/ T H R E E /

"What the hell is going on over there?" Sam Hartley said to his friend Kevin.

Kevin, who was a far cry from observant, asked, "Over where?"

"Over there by that park bench," Sam said with annoyance. "Something weird is going on. I think we should go check it out."

"What are you talking about, Sam? There's nothing weird going on. It looks to me like some woman is sitting on the ground by a tree. What's the big deal?" Then Kevin's voice took on a sinister tone. "Oooh, look out, everybody. Some scary secretary is out sitting under a tree enjoying the first sunshine we've had in months. What sort of unspeakable horror is she busy conjuring? Maybe she'll terrorize the world by eating a peanut butter and jelly sandwich. Oh, the horror! Oh, the humanity!"

"Ok, I get it, Kevin. Your sarcastic wit has not fallen on deaf ears. But tell me what that is next to her. It looks like a man lying on his back; maybe he's dead."

"Oh yeah, I'm sure. Every person lying in the grass enjoying the sunshine is dead. Sam, you better do something about that wild imagination of yours."

"Fine, Kevin, fine. I know I have an active imagination—big freaking deal. You can say whatever you want, but I'm telling you, something weird is going on over there. I'm going over to see what's what."

"Knock yourself out, Sammy boy. I'll be sitting here on my bench, soaking in rays and relaxing. After you've discovered that all of this was in your head, come back, and we'll enjoy the rest of our lunch hour."

Sam walked across the park toward the woman under the tree. As he got closer, he heard what sounded like the distant, tinny voice of someone speaking over a phone. It was coming from the grass, not far from the woman. Then he heard the woman herself, almost chanting in some strange dialect he has never heard before.

She slowly rocked back and forth, mumbling in her bizarre language, "Quavilla esto monalinko dazaflog."

As he reached the woman, Sam noticed the other body lying in the grass. It appeared to be that of a man, but Sam couldn't be sure, as the thing's face was unrecognizable. Even its head was cracked open, and its brains pooled in the grass. Sam could hear the buzzing of hundreds of blowflies, making him wonder what sort of communication allowed them to find death so quickly.

In the distance, he saw yet another body, this one was as faceless as the last, but it appeared less damaged than the other. Sam didn't know why, but for some reason, he thought of facial surgery. Then he noticed the buildings across from the park disgorging what looked like hundreds of workers who had chosen not to skip out a bit early as he and Kevin had. They were about to get the shock of their lives.

What in the hell was going on? What had happened to these people, and why was this woman sitting alone, mumbling? That was when he noticed the two blackbirds bouncing through the grass toward the woman.

One of the birds pecked at something lying in the woman's open palm. Sam's stomach clenched with disgust as he saw the bird hop away with a human eyeball dangling from the muscles and filaments it held tightly in its beak. The orb swung back and forth like a pendulum, dripping tiny droplets of blood in its wake. Sam released an audible gasp, and the woman turned to face him.

She shouted her gibberish now, "Mololla dero Banga harawan!"

That was when Sam saw the hollow black and crimson orifices that had once held the woman's eyes. Deep furrows dug into her cheeks ran down from the empty sockets acting like tributaries for the blood streaming down her ruined face. The woman's non-seeing face turned toward the sound of Sam's presence, and as she broke into a large, happy grin, her hands reached up, fingers sliding inside her mouth, each hand grabbing tightly onto the bottom jaw. With the sound of breaking bones serving as the soundtrack for this heinous ballet of the bizarre, Sam watched in paralytic horror as the woman began twisting and tearing at her lower jaw. At first, she broke it free of its physical moorings, then eventually pulling it entirely away from her face itself in a flurry of torn flesh, broken bones, and a shower of blood.

She fell sideways, collapsing to the ground in a heap as Sam reached her. But there would be no assistance he could render. She convulsed for a few seconds then all movement ceased.

Sam began to cry, something he hadn't done since he was a kid. He whispered a prayer, which was something else he hadn't done in longer than he could recall. But partway into his plea, his words became a garbled mess of incomprehensible babbling.

/ F O U R /

As Kevin sat meditating, he heard a growing series of noises coming from the park's far end. He couldn't make out what anyone was saying, but he knew that something terrible was happening by the tone of the voices. Concerned about what sort of trouble his friend Sam might have gotten himself into, Kevin looked out in the distance and was staggered by what he saw. There were dozens, no hundreds of people in the park, all screaming, waving their arms, and attacking each other. People were punching, kicking, and gouging each other in some of the most violent acts Kevin had ever imagined. Many of the people appeared to be inflicting pain upon themselves as well. He saw people tearing the flesh from their faces. He saw others ripping arms out of people's sockets then using them as clubs to beat more people.

It was complete insanity. It was the sort of thing Sam might imagine but not Kevin. Not only did his thought never travel to such places, but he was having great trouble wrapping his head around the reality he was now seeing. Sam was out there amid that horror, and Kevin had no way of finding him. What in the hell could have caused so many people to lose their minds and begin slaughtering each other, not to mention maiming themselves?

As he turned to run, Kevin said to himself, "Ok. I may not be smart enough to know what's going on over there, but I do know if I want to stay alive, I have to get out of here and pronto. Maybe if I can get far enough away, I can call . . . I can call . . . I . . . ironda maradunga banadogo. . . ."

WORMS

"Worms!" John Alexander shouted as he brought the point of his spade down on the squirming creature cleaving it neatly in two wriggling halves. Then he turned the spade with the flat bottom facing down and began to smash at the soil shouting angrily with each subsequent thrust. "I . . . hate . . . these stinking . . . slithering . . . dirt-crawling . . . things."

By the time he stopped, the two formerly twitching earthworm halves were gone from sight, likely still gyrating somewhere under the soil. John needed to get this work done before the next rainfall. If not, he knew what would happen then. There would be more of them, dozens, perhaps hundreds of the dreadful creatures crawling and slithering about his walk and driveway. He should have known better. He should have realized this before he built his home here. If so, he never would have done so. What the hell had he been thinking?

The land beneath John Alexander's subdivision was originally quite fertile. It was some of the richest farmland in Western Berks County, Pennsylvania. Although several feet of the fertile topsoil had been scraped off and resold by the developer, there was still about six inches of good earth resting atop a base of unforgiving clay.

One of the things John discovered rather quickly and found disturbing was the abundance of earthworms in the thin layer of dirt. Even though John understood the essential role worms played in aerating the soil and keeping it healthy, it did little to assuage his feelings. He hated the wretched creatures; he had always hated them his entire life. In John's mind, the only thing more revolting than the slimy things burrowing underground was the thought of the same disgusting critters were crawling over his flesh.

Some might consider his semi-phobia irrational; however, John didn't. When he was a child, he often recalled the older boys telling stories about how when you died, the worms came to feast on your body as it moldered in the grave. They even made up disgusting songs and rhymes about it chanting, "The worms crawl in, the worms crawl out, the green saliva comes out of your mouth." It didn't matter to John that the worms in these childhood poems were larvae and maggots. In his young mind, earthworms, larvae, or inchworms were all the same. He hated them all.

He often had nightmares of being buried and trapped naked inside a rotting wooden coffin, stinking of moisture, mold, and decay. He recalled how real everything seemed in these dreams as the cold, slime-covered creatures slinked over his exposed flesh. He always woke up at the same point in the nightmare, covered in sweat and panting like a dog after a long run. That was when the worms began to crawl over his lips, into his mouth, and slide down his throat.

As an adult, John found himself still plagued not only by dreaded thoughts of the horrible slimy things, but he now lived in a house surrounded by soil that was teaming with them. He learned this unfortunate bit of information following the first prolonged, heavy rainfall. That morning, while walking out to his car John noticed a particularly odd fishy odor. He looked down, and to his shock, John discovered his driveway covered with dozens of disgusting earthworms of all shapes and sizes. At first, he stood staring down at the horrible sight. Some were short and fat. Others long stretched out to nearly seven inches; all disgusting, all wriggling.

He considered getting his garden hose and blasting his driveway clean but realized the disgusting things would puddle at the bottom of the driveway, and that might be even more disgusting. John learned the best way to get to the safety of his car was to tiptoe carefully between the squirming creatures. He succeeded in doing so, scarcely managing to keep his breakfast in his stomach in the process. At one point, John stepped on an exceptionally thick and juicy critter, feeling it squish beneath his shoe. As he got his car door, open John scrapped his shoe on a bare spot in the driveway, eager to get the remains free of his sole.

As he drove through his neighborhood, John noticed every street and every driveway was in the same repulsive condition as his own. He felt as if the fishy stench was stuck in his sinuses and might linger there all day. His car rolled over worm after worm. He could only imagine what his tires and wheel wells must look like with dozens of wiggling half-dead worm carcasses dangling from them. The thought made his stomach lurch. He stopped at a twenty-four-hour automatic car wash on his way to work. He hated to spend the money, but he had no intention of either looking at the mess on his tires or washing the creatures off by himself.

That particular event had taken place several weeks earlier, and to his pleasure, after that, it had been a dry spring. As such, a similar heavy rain had not occurred since. However, he made up his mind by the time the next heavy rain came, his driveway would be worm-free. There was little he could do about the rest of his neighborhood or its streets, but at least he could try to stop the problem at his own home.

John began researching the elimination of earthworms from his lawn and found quite an abundance of helpful information. He learned that simply adding a bird feeder to his front yard might attract robins and other birds to eat the worms. He wasn't sure he wanted to go that route, however, as the thought of dozens of birds crapping all over his car was not much more appealing than the worms themselves.

He read that worms thrive in moist soil. If he didn't water his lawn, the number of worms might diminish. But his yard was still relatively new, and he didn't want to have to pay to have it reseeded if it dried out and the grass died. He also learned about pesticides and "chemical vermifuges," such as potassium permanganate and formalin. John felt as though he was reading in some foreign language, which he supposed he was. He also wasn't crazy about these chemicals since the literature said they didn't kill the worms but brought them out of the soil so he could sweep them away. The idea of his sweeping hundreds of worms down his driveway was more disgusting than stepping over them or using the hose on them.

When he was about to give up, John found some pesticides that he was sure would kill all the worms in his lawn.

Fortunately, he had no pets or children as the warnings said the poison might prove harmful to them. He did give some momentary consideration to the birds, squirrels, and other wildlife in his area but decided his need to eliminate the worms was too great, and they would have to either survive or not on their own.

"Survival of the fittest," he said, "Darwin, baby, Darwin."

John purchased the necessary pesticide and generously spread it on his lawn as instructed, feeling confident that his driveway would be worm-free by the next heavy rainfall.

Periodically during the first several days after the initial application of the pesticide, John did find the occasional dead bird, chipmunk, or even stray cat on his lawn. As repulsed as he was by the discoveries, he somehow gathered the necessary strength to relegate the carcasses to his trash tub for weekly collection. He felt a bit like a ghoul lurking about in the dark, shoveling up the remains, stuffing them into a plastic garbage bag, then depositing them into his large trash receptacle.

Within a week or two, the animal deaths seemed to have stopped, and John assumed the pesticide had done its job. He supposed he'd find out soon. There were heavy summer rains predicted for the upcoming weekend. To everyone's surprise, not only was the rainstorm intense, but it was much more severe than anyone had anticipated and lasted for most of the weekend. Late that Sunday evening, John periodically went to his front window and looked at the driving rain as it pounded his neighborhood, sending deep streams of water cascading down the sides of his street while the storm drains struggled to keep flowing. John decided there was nothing for him to do but go to bed. He could check the status of his driveway early Monday morning when he left for work.

When he awoke, he noticed the rain had stopped, and it was an unusually still, quiet morning. He got ready for work then went out to survey the status of his driveway. To his pleasure, he saw the blacktop was completely clear and free of any worms. He could still smell a fishy scent in the air and had assumed the roads and everyone else's driveway had their share of the disgusting creatures. At least he had won his war against nature.

As he walked toward his car, John heard a strange wet sloshing sound. It reminded him of the sound a garden hose made when being pulled through wet leaves and grass. Then the fishy scent became even more intense. He turned and looked out into the early morning darkness at the street beyond. In the glow of the nearby streetlight, he saw something happening, which he knew was impossible.

Detritus from the storm covered the street. Branches, leaves, trash, undefinable refuse were everywhere. And worms, lots and lots of worms, all alive and squirming among the debris. Suddenly an icy fear stabbed its knives into John's belly. The mass of rubble in the street was some-how impossibly coming together, layer upon layer building higher and higher, all the while appearing to form something resembling a semi-humanoid shape.

"Golem" was the word that popped into John's mind. John had read about the mythical creatures of folklore which created themselves from dirt or mud. That was what he was seeing brought to life at the end of his driveway. The thing had grown to well over twelve feet tall, and even in the limited light, John could see the beast was being held into its form by thousands of squirming earthworms.

The hell-spawned beast turned its head in John's direction as it raised its arms high in the air. It opened its mouth and let loose with an ear-splitting, foul-smelling roar that shook John to the very core of his being. For a moment, he stood in shocked paralysis until the creature lifted its leg and dropped it to the wet street with a great pounding thump, which vibrated through John's body. It was then he knew why this Golem was there. It had come for him. The very creatures John had tried to eliminate now formed the beast.

Realizing the extent of his plight, John jumped into his car, slammed the door shut, put the car in reverse, and flew down the driveway determined to smash the monster back into the debris from which it arose. His vehicle slammed into the legs of the creature sending a shock wave through John's body. Then it stalled. He tried to restart it, but it wouldn't turn over. Looking in his rearview mirror, John saw as he had predicted the Golem had fallen to pieces. However, he hadn't anticipated what would happen next. The fragments of rubbish fell to the surface of his car and clung to it, rapidly forming a creeping shell around the vehicle.

The windows had become a thick opaque mass of remnants from the creature. Looking at the windshield, John saw bits of fur, feathers, and in some cases, complete carcasses of dead animals floating among the army of thousands of wriggling, squirming worms. Then the smell hit him like a slap in the face. It was the stench of dead animals, wet rotting leaves, and the fishy reek of worms.

He heard the sound of metal creaking as the cocoon began to tighten itself around the car. Then the first crack appeared in his windshield, followed by another, then another. Soon the car was filling with squirming, debris and John found himself up to his neck in the vile compost. He tried fruitlessly to get his door open. John desperately held his lips tightly together as the crawling mass slid all over his face. But when the worms began to climb into his nostrils, John found he had no choice but to breathe through his mouth. The nightmares of his suddenly became a reality as creatures squirmed over his lips and slithered down his throat. However, there would be no awakening from this horror.

BAIT AND SWITCH

"Bait the hook well. The fish will bite."

—William Shakespeare

"Do not bite at the bait of pleasure, till you know there is no hook beneath it." —Thomas Jefferson

"Look up ahead. There's bait active around that bend. We're bound to catch something good up there," the young girl said to her friend.

They were in the process of playing the latest and hottest augmented reality game known as Monster Mayhem. The game was just one of a dozen such games attracting a worldwide audience of gamers and making its developers millions of dollars. The competition required its players to go out into parks and other places to "capture" various digital monsters that appeared randomly. The couple was presently playing in a local museum park, and the sun was sinking low in the western sky.

There, of course, were all sorts of rules and a variety of weapons available to help capture the monsters. One such tool called "setting bait" allowed the player to place bait around one of the digital markers to attract monsters to that particular location.

"Yeah, but look around, Jill. It's getting dark, and there are no lights out this far."

"Seriously, Seth? Are you trying to tell me you're afraid of the dark?"

Seth found himself in a quandary. He liked Jill a lot. He hoped she might soon stop thinking of him as just a friend and maybe allow their relationship to take a more romantic turn. Perhaps this was just another teenage fantasy, but he was attracted to Jill. However, if he showed signs of being anything less than manly or protective, that opportunity might never come.

"Of course, I'm not! I'm not afraid of anything. It's just getting harder to see the path with just the minimal light from our phones. We left the blacktop a while back, and this path is nothing but dirt and gravel. I'm concerned you might trip, fall and hurt yourself."

"I'll be fine, Seth. Don't worry about me. Look, this is a city park, and there are dozens of people around here playing the game just like we are."

"I know, but they're far behind us now in the main part of the park where the light is. Nobody's way out here."

"Somebody is. Look at that bait on the screen Seth. That means someone had to set it up and he's likely out there right now getting tons of great monsters while we're standing here in the dark arguing. The clock is ticking, Seth. Baits are only good for like a half-hour, and we have no idea how long this one has been running."

Seth looked at his cell phone, "Oh great!"

"What?"

"Look at the name of the guy who set up the bait."

Jill looked at her phone and said, "It says 'Player Slayer.' So what?"

"Doesn't that nickname bother you? I mean, if this was a horror movie, we'd be screaming at the screen for the characters to turn tail and run. That name doesn't concern you even a little bit?"

"No, of course not. We all have goofy nicknames. Yours is 'Ultra Balls 2.' Tell me that isn't just a little bit vain."

"You know it isn't. I just took the name from the Ultra Balls we use in the game. That's all."

"Sure, you did. Now stop being so weird, Seth. Now let's go over there and see what we can catch."

"Fine, fine. But as soon as we get our share of monsters, we're heading back to civilization. Deal?"

"Sure, it's a deal. Now let's hurry."

The pair made their way along the path toward the area where the program's GPS screen showed the location of the bait. As they followed a curve in the walk, they came upon an open space with a wooden bench. There was no one in sight.

"This is the spot. Let's see what shows up," Jill suggested.

"Nobody's here, Jill. I wonder why 'Player Slayer' set the bait and then didn't stick around?"

"Geese, Seth. Stop worrying about dumb stuff. He could have set them up and gotten bored waiting for monsters to show up and just left. You know, some people have no patience, and sometimes it seems to take forever for monsters to be attracted to the bait. Look at your sightings bar, and you can see there are a couple of them nearby."

Seth looked down at his phone and said sarcastically. "Oh wow. Big fat deal! A Megadon, a Sykill and a

Wolyhump. Boring! No wonder the guy abandoned this location. You can get those things all over the place and without wasting a single bait chip."

"Whatever, Seth. We're here, so let's give it a few minutes and see what else shows up?"

"Alright. But as soon as the bait runs down, we head back. Ok."

"Ok fine. Just stop bugging me about it. You're starting to work on my nerves."

Seth didn't reply. He knew Jill well enough to understand she was about to lose her temper, and she did have quite a spirited one indeed. Seth was starting to wonder if maybe his idea about making Jill his girlfriend was a bad idea after all. He had known her since they were toddlers. They had been together in every grade in school. That closeness combined with his raging hormones and Jill's blossoming figure and good looks had been the reason for his thoughts to turn to romance in the first place. But maybe he needed to rethink this course of action. She could be a real pain in the butt sometimes.

"Come on, Jill. This is a waste of time. Let's go."

"Ok, but just give it a minute. Something's bound to show up. I mean, come on. That's the whole purpose of setting bait in the first place."

"That's only partially true," A voice suddenly said from out of the darkness.

Instinctively, Jill reached over and grabbed Seth's hand. He felt warmth spread throughout his body at the excitement of her touch. Yet the fear, which was simultaneously shooting through him, overshadowed his momentary pleasure. He lifted his phone in the direction of the voice for light but couldn't see anyone there.

The voice continued, "Yes. You can set the bait to attract monsters for you to hunt in your game. But bait can also serve other purposes."

A pair of legs clothed in dark black jeans and dark boots stepped into the light of Seth's phone. Seth raised the light slowly along the stranger's body and saw the man wore a black tee-shirt and a long black leather coat. He had on a dark black wide-brimmed hat, which shielded his downturned face. But Seth could see the man had a heavy black beard.

"You know, a lot of people think this whole Monster Mayhem game is just a fad and is stupid and ridiculous. In some ways, they may be right. However, I've discovered these sorts of games can serve many good purposes. They get people, especially kids, off the sofa. You can't be a couch potato and play these games. You have to get up and get out of the house. I'm sure you're aware we have become such a sedentary society. The players get to walk around and get good exercise while enjoying an interesting game. They also get to meet and interact with other players in real life, face-to-face rather than sitting at home in front of some video screen talking to unseen players over a headset. I think those are all good things. Wouldn't you agree?"

Neither of them responded. Jill squeezed Seth's hand even tighter. The man raised his head, and Seth heard Jill gasp next to him. Scars rippled the stranger's face appearing as if he had survived a bad burn and his eyes seemed to glow with an intensity that suggested a madness living somewhere deep within him. The man opened his mouth in a deranged smile, revealing a maw filled with brown and rotting teeth. He barely looked human at all. He was more like one of the monsters from the game.

"But you see, bait can also serve another purpose. You can use bait to attract game players like the both of you. And as my game name Player-Slayer suggests, I enjoy hunting you much more than the fictional game characters."

The last thing Jill and Seth saw in their young lives was the long, sharp sword blade glimmering in the light from their cell phones as the weapon of death came slashing down toward them.

SUB SANDWICHES

The two businessmen walked casually along the street, heading toward the area of the city known for its casual dining. The noonday sun warmed their faces making the spring day seem more like summer.

"I don't know what to do, Bob. This project has the potential of allowing us to sell many thousands of units. Right now, the factory is almost operating at full capacity. And with summer right around the corner, folks will be taking vacations, and others won't be willing to give up their weekends to work, even for overtime pay."

"Yeah, I know, Jim, but how the hell can we say no to such a great opportunity. And don't forget the high-profit margins we have on these components. It's a real money-maker. Besides, you know we always find some way to pull a rabbit out of our hats. I realize we must design, manufacture, assemble, and test the units, but I honestly think we can do it. Tell me. How many units do you think we can handle per month without risking our current customer orders? And be honest; don't be too conservative or over-ambitious either. I need to get a realistic feel here."

Jim thought for a moment, then said, "I honestly think we can push out another one to two hundred a month, but that's nowhere near the five to six hundred the customer is requesting."

Being the experienced salesman he was, Bob assured Jim saying, "Well, you leave that up to me. I think I can get the customer to accept, let's say, two hundred the first month with the right amount of persuasion. We can follow that with a fifty unit increase each month until we eventually find a way to get to four or five hundred per month by the end of the order."

"Wow! If you could pull that off, I honestly think we could find a way to make this work."

Before Jim finished his thoughts, a frantically running man slammed into him, practically knocking him to the ground. Jim managed to grab onto Bob for support. Lying on the ground, dressed in tattered rags that might have once been clothing, the wild man mumbled gibberish through his tongue-less mouth as he lay on the ground holding painfully onto his damaged leg.

"Don't worry gentlemen, we have him," a voice called from behind as two hulking uniformed men brandishing Tasers fell on the runner rendering him unconscious with fifty thousand volts of electricity.

"Thank you both so much," Jim said, startled.

"We're so sorry. This one got loose on us. Were either of you injured?" The concerned soldier asked.

Bob replied, "No, no, we're fine. Thanks. Just a bit shook up, is all."

"Damned freak, stinking subhuman," the other soldier replied, "I hate these bastards. Our bosses have us cut their tongues out so they can't shout and carry on, but I wish they'd let us hobble them so they couldn't run away."

With no further discussion, the two soldiers dragged the unconscious man away to a waiting recovery vehicle.

"Thank goodness you're all right, Jim. Do you realize what that creature could have done to you if he'd gotten a good grip on you?"

"Yeah, I do. Thank goodness the creature couldn't bite me. The handlers do still remove their teeth, don't they?"

"As far as I know, they do," Bob replied, "I believe they started doing that a few years ago after a few unpleasant and unfortunate incidents."

Jim said, "Yeah. Remember how it was back then, with these things roaming the streets, homeless, crazy, mumbling incoherently, and constantly bothering people?"

"Yep. And a good many of those people were dangerous as well," Bob said. Then he pointed up the street. "Hey, look, up ahead. What say we hit Gino's Deli for a couple of sub sandwiches? I realize you might not have much of an appetite after that encounter, but if you don't eat now, you'll be starving by this afternoon."

"Yeah, I suppose you're right. I should eat something."

As the pair approached the door to the deli, they heard the sound of a truck coming down the busy street. They saw it was a sizeable flat-bed style vehicle with a series of long open-barred crates stacked five high and a dozen deep all along both sides of the truck bed. As the truck got closer, they recognized one of the many inhabitants of the crates lying flat, staring out at the pedestrians with a dazed expression, twitching, spasmodically, every few seconds.

"Hey, isn't that the guy who almost knocked me down?" Jim said.

"Yeah, he won't be knocking anyone else down any time soon."

"You know Bob; even though I understand the necessity, I don't think I'll ever get used to seeing human beings caged in those crates."

"I know what you mean, but it's just something we have to accept. You can't think of those creatures as human beings either. They aren't the same as us, not by a long shot. It's how the government decided to handle a troublesome situation. Think about it this way; you love the taste of beef and chicken? But you have no desire to kill the animals yourself or go to a slaughterhouse to see the work in progress, right?"

Jim said, "Right, but who is it that makes the determination, you know, who decides who will go in the cages and who won't?"

"Why the government, of course, and their experts."

Looking around as if to make sure no one was listening, Jim asked, "But don't you ever wonder if maybe some normal people who might have pissed off the wrong people in charge could end up on one of those trucks?"

"No, I don't believe so, Jim. We have to trust our government to do what's right for us. They watch out for us and protect us. Without the government, where would we be?"

"Yeah. I suppose you're right. Still, it's the sort of thing that's open for abuse with the wrong people in charge, don't you think?"

"No, not really, Jim. I'm sure there are a series of checks and balances in the process to make sure nothing goes wrong. Remember when it all first was proposed by the government so many years ago? It was a bit weird for those of us who were already adults, but now a generation later, our kids just accept it. To them, it's perfectly normal."

"I suppose so. But those trucks look like the old chicken trucks from back when we were kids. The one that they used to haul hundreds of chickens to slaughter."

"Yeah, I know. But that was a different time and a whole different situation. I wonder, where do you suppose those trucks are going? Do you think they're heading off to the camps, or maybe they're going for processing?"

Jim thought for a moment, then said, "Don't know, and I suppose I shouldn't care. I prefer not to think about it anymore. Let's go get our subs."

The pair entered the deli, smelling the unique aromas of cooking meat. Taking their place in line, Jim looked behind the counter where a large, browned slab was cooking, rotating on a spit over an open gas flame—wielding a gleaming carving knife, one of the butchers cut off a thin slice just behind the neck stump where its head used to be.

"Wow, it smells incredible in here. I think I'm getting my appetite back," Jim said.

Bob agreed, "Yeah, me too."

They saw the sign hanging overhead as they approached the counter and seemed to pay it little interest. The sign read, "Subhuman sandwiches. The best in town."

WHAT IS A MAN?

"The good man is the friend of all living things."

—Mahatma Gandhi

"It is not death that a man should fear, but he should fear never beginning to live."   —Marcus Aurelius

"Death may be the greatest of all human blessings."

—Socrates

The massive creature sat silently, hunched on the chill, damp cave floor. The beast listened to the hypnotic drip, drip, dripping of water somewhere deep in the blackness, painstaking forming stalactites and stalagmites as it had done for millions of years before. He could hear the steady thump, thump, thumping of his own oversized heart sounding like the rhythmic beating of tribal drums echoing in his mind as the water reverberated in the near silence of the cavern.

Lining the walls surrounding him were bookshelves reaching ten feet tall, overflowing with thousands of volumes containing the most significant writings in human history. Wooden creates and skids held stacks upon stacks of even more books; classic fiction, historical accounts, religious essays, and scientific journals. He had read them all, most more than once. He had acquired them over many years, and they were among his most prized possessions.

In the darkness of a nearby alcove, an old-fashioned gramophone complete with hand crank stood ready for use along with stacks of hundreds of classic orchestral albums. When not reading, the creature loved to listen to music. On any available wall space remaining in the cavern, not occupied by bookshelves, priceless works of art by some great masters and ancient tapestries hung for his viewing pleasure.

Near his feet, a small collection of hot coals burned, the remnants of his former fire. He would rebuild the fire again soon, not for heat but for light so that he might read throughout the night. Presently, his massive muscular arms rested on his knees, allowing his shovel-sized hands to dangle down over tree-trunk-like legs. His bucket-sized head hung low as his chin rested on his barrel chest below massive shoulders more than five feet across. Although the cave was quite cold, the chilly temperatures never bothered him.

The monstrous hulking creature might appear to have been sleeping to an uninformed onlooker, but he was not. He never slept because he didn't need to sleep. He hadn't slept in years, perhaps decades. This particular restive position was the closest he ever came to sleeping. He thought of it as his thinking pose, and although his frightening physical appearance might suggest otherwise, the thinking was what he enjoyed doing most.

He suddenly sat bolt upright, his eyes glowing like the embers in his fire. He remained motionless now, silent in the shadows, carefully listening to the shuffling noise coming from the front of the cave near the entrance. He immediately recognized the familiar gate he had heard so many times before. It was another one of those wretched things; the dead ones. Somehow one of the creatures must have inadvertently found its way into his cave. Adam could feel his anger growing. How dare this abomination enter his home! He would be sure to guarantee this encounter would not end well for the intruder.

Adam wondered how many of those mindless shambling creatures remained in the world. Hundreds of them? Perhaps thousands? Possibly millions? He suspected millions might be an accurate assumption from a national perspective, but maybe only a few hundred locally. Humankind had done an exemplary job of eradicating the monsters over the past twelve years.

The shambling creature slowly made its way across the cave and into the minimal light cast by the dwindling fire. Adam studied the thing carefully. It appeared to have once been a male, but decomposition had taken its toll, which made distinguishing its gender almost impossible. Its clothing was in tatters, and it made that same low guttural growl they all made. The vile stench coming off the unholy beast was beyond appalling. This one had been decomposing for quite some time.

Adam knew well what these undead creatures, these zombies did whenever they encountered living humans. They ripped their victims to pieces, devouring their flesh and innards. He fumed at the very notion of one of these wretched things tromping about in his home, his anger continuing to grow.

The undead monster advanced, stumbling about the cave, apparently unaware of his presence. Adam stood and rose to his full height of eight feet, yet still, the creature ignored him. Then again, they always ignored him. It seemed like he was invisible to them. This phenomenon, too, caused him incredible frustration. Perhaps for personal reasons, he felt it better not to consider why he was so angry.

He bellowed in a booming angry voice, "Do you not see me, you disgusting pile of rotting meat? Here I am, standing right before you. Am I not made of human flesh and blood? Do you not wish to partake of my body, you revolting spawn of Hell?"

The zombie stood and stared, not so much at Adam as through him. It was like the zombie was confused, uncertain as to what his next move should be. Adam believed the creature could hear him shouting but, for whatever reason, couldn't sense him. He had tried this experiment on the undead countless times with the same futile results, and it was becoming maddening. Who was it who had said the definition of insanity was repeating the same thing over and over but expecting different results? Adam couldn't recall, but the recollection was making him question his sanity.

A low moan came from the zombie's throat, sounding not so much threatening as bewildered. It started to turn away. With one mighty swipe of his muscular arm, Adam severed the creature's head from its body, sending the skull flying across the cave and slamming into a wall with a sickening crack. The body thudded to the cave floor. He wasn't sure exactly why separating the head from the body or why, by simply making the brain inactive, killed the creatures; he just knew it worked.

He had accidentally discovered this fact many years earlier, more out of frustration than through any scientific process. He has come upon one of the monsters in the forest. It was a huge male, not as large as himself but still quite threatening in appearance. At that time, Adam was not only unaware the dead were reanimating, he also didn't know that they paid him no mind. He thought the creature was a living, breathing man and, therefore, a potential enemy. His natural assumption was to believe the monster would try to attack him. After all, anyone coming upon him his entire life would attack first and ask questions later.

Reaching out, Adam had grabbed onto the thing's left arm and pulled it from the socket. To his shock, no blood spurted from the stump, only a slight trickle of some viscous, puss-like fluid leaked out. The creature didn't seem even to notice his injury. Eager to end the encounter, Adam thrust his long arm outward toward his opponent's chest, penetrating his flesh with surprising ease and pulling out what he assumed would be his attacker's still-beating heart.

To his dismay, Adam held a dead gray, bloodless thing that teamed with maggots in its advanced stage of decomposition. And still, the creature stood. It looked down at the hole in its chest for a moment, then let out a deep growing sound. Frustrated and unsure what to do next, Adam bent down, retrieved the severed arm, then swinging it like a war club, he struck the creature's head. Its spinal column snapped with an audible crack, causing it to fall to the ground. He test-kicked the mass of flesh, and it remained inanimate.

He made a mental note that if he ever came upon a creature such as this again, the head, probably the brainstem, would be the weak link. Little did he know he would battle many more of the beasts in the years that followed.

Now, Adam bent down, grabbing this latest zombie's foot and dragging it toward the entrance of the cave. Then like a slow-moving soccer player, he used one of his own giant feet to pass the severed head along as well. At the cave entrance, Adam kicked the skull hard, sending it flying for several hundred feet out through the night and into the darkness of the forest.

Still holding the zombie's foot, he began to swing the corpse around and around, gaining velocity so he could fling the disgusting thing as far away as possible. During one of the rotations, the corpse took off, flying hundreds of yards out into the darkness. Adam realized the body had taken off before he had let go. He looked down and saw the thing's foot with exposed ankle bones jutting from tatters of moldering flesh still in his giant hand. He threw the foot as far away as possible with disgust and then wiped his hand on his pants.

His cave, the place Adam called home, was located high up on the side of a mountain hidden by countless pine trees. He hoped the stench accompanying the vile creatures would not be noticeable, but he had his doubts. He recalled a time not that long ago when the entire world stank of rotting flesh. Now the creatures were few and far between. These days, humans thought of them more as a nuisance than a threat.

He sniffed the air and could smell burning wood, not the scent of a nearby campfire but something much more intense. He looked out into the distance to where he knew a good-sized town stood many miles away. He could see the orange glow of a fire burning out of control.

"I can't believe they are at it again," he thought. "When will these people ever learn?"

Even now, after surviving a plague that practically wiped out humanity, these humans still felt the need to be at war. It was like people could only be satisfied if they were killing. And it didn't matter if they were killing zombies or one another. He recalled several years after the initial outbreak when the then newly reformed federal government began offering the general public the opportunity to collect bounty money by killing zombies. Although the program had an official name, people began referring to it as a Dead Kill bounty; the idea being that you were killing something, which was already dead. Survivors suddenly realized instead of running and hiding from these deadly monsters, they could earn a decent living by killing them. That was the beginning of the end for the undead. Soon what was once an ocean of roaming undead became a river, then a stream, and finally just a trickle, a fraction of what they had once been.

More than ten years since the dreaded Zombie Virus of 2043, also known as the Z43 Virus, started the zombie apocalypse. Yet now, years after the so-called zombie wars, humanity was still killing his fellow man, even though the act of doing so created more living dead. The Z43 virus still existed inside every living human, remaining dormant until the time of death when it activated. Years earlier, the government created preventive measures to dispose of any new deceased properly. These measures prevented the dead from returning. But in the case of war, there was no guarantee all the dead could be accounted for and would remain deceased. There was an excellent chance whatever skirmish had just occurred in that city miles away would create new monsters rising from the ashes.

It troubled Adam how humans still seemed to have this need to kill each other. From his observations, there were two facets of human survivors: the so-called civilized people who lived safely behind the walls of fortified cities and those called outlanders who lived like lawless savages in the wilderness outside the cities. The outlanders had turned their backs on civilized society in favor of a life free of legal restraints. The outlanders set up their cultures like tribes, with the most potent members leading the groups. Without laws to control their behavior for more than a decade, these survivors lived like savages, not unlike those not seen since the dawn of man. Most had even abandoned formal language, replacing it with monosyllabic gibberish nearly unintelligible. Not only were these outlanders at constant war with the humans inside the cities, but rival tribes constantly fought among themselves.

Adam wondered with a heavy heart just how many humans of both factions might have died in this latest conflict. The world had become a much different place than the one he had once known. So much had changed since his birth in 1792, or perhaps re-birth would be a better description. It was a hard fact to comprehend now in 2055, more than two and a half centuries later.

Adam didn't know if he carried the Z43 virus. True he was a man, but not a man like other men. He was not only different but unique. Perhaps this made him immune to the virus. It seemed to make him uninteresting to the dead ones, so maybe that idea might be accurate. Or it might be the circumstances of his creation that caused the walking corpses to leave him alone. He wasn't sure, but he hoped someday to find an answer. He suddenly heard groaning noises coming from the forest far off to his right. He realized more of the undead creatures must have followed the first.

His night vision was exceptional, and the bright moon further helped him see them coming. There were ten or more of the zombies in this cluster. If he simply stood still, Adam knew they would ignore him and walk by, but that would never do. They might find their way into his cave and fill it with their revolting stink. His shelter was not much, but it was his home and had been for decades. He could not allow these things to defile his domicile.

Adam charged headlong into the mass of rotting walking corpses using arms, legs, hands, and feet to dismantle the creatures. In a mad frenzy of savage destruction, Adam cut his way through the crowd, leaving not one of them standing.

One of the creatures had shuffled toward Adam, appearing to try to pass through him like he wasn't there. Adam slammed his massive hands against both sides of the zombie's head in a thunderous clap, sending brains exploding out of the creature's squashed mouth and eye sockets, like someone stomping on an open tube of toothpaste.

Two others were staggering about aimlessly. Adam raced at them, driving his fist through the face of the first monster and out the back of the creature's head. He pulled his muscular arm back, and the head separated from the thing's body but remained stuck on his hand. Adam slammed the decapitated head into the skull of the other zombie, succeeding in breaking that creature's neck and cracking open the zombie skull attached to his massive hand.

Two more zombies stumbled into view, one male and the other female. Adam walked up to them, palming their heads like an NBA all-star. He lifted them both up by their skulls more than two feet off the ground as they squirmed and struggled to get free. Then he began to close his hands, squeezing ever tighter. Within seconds their skulls crushed inward, sending shards of broken bones deep into their decomposing brains. Puss and grey matter oozed onto Adam's fingers.

After finishing the remainder of the herd in a fashion equally repulsive, Adam decided it was time to clean up. He tossed the remains into the woods to join those of the others. This cleanup was a challenging task not only because of the number of creatures Adam had slaughtered but because of the savage way he had dismembered them. He expected such carnage after he found himself in the throes of a rampage. The forest floor looked like a charnel house.

Adam stood for a moment, smelling the disgusting stench of the beasts. He looked down at his hands and clothing finding them covered in blood, puss, and bits of flesh from his savage onslaught. Adam needed to get clean. Walking along a path he knew well, Adam made his way through the woods to a lake where he stripped naked a waded into the shallows to rinse both himself and his clothing. His flesh, a patchwork of thousands of scars connecting flesh of varying hues, seemed iridescent in the moonlight. He examined himself for injuries but found none.

Seeing himself bared to the world made Adam think about his past and his life. He recalled as he often did about the man he thought of as his father. That man had been a scientist. No, he had been much more than a scientist; he had been a creator, a genius, and in Adam's opinion, a god. Yet, he had also been a cold-hearted, unfeeling man who had rejected Adam and hated him. Adam found it more than ironic that he should possess a kinder heart and more respect for humanity than the man responsible for giving him life.

He wondered not for the first time, what exactly was humanity? What is a man? Was he, himself not a man? Indeed, he must be as he was made from man. His father and creator had seen to that. And was he, Adam, not a good man? He considered himself an intellectual, perhaps not at the level of genius his father had attained. Still, he was knowledgeable and possessed a love for art, science, mathematics, music, and literature.

He was generally kind to his fellow man. Yes, he had killed in the past, both zombies and living humans as well. Early on, his killing had been out of frustration, rage, ignorance, and misunderstanding. Later he learned to control his impulses and kill only in self-defense.

His father had not thought of him as intelligent, just the opposite. He had even refused to give Adam a name, referring to him instead as "the monster," "the wretch," "the ogre," and other such derogatory terms. And when news of his existence became public, the townspeople had called him "an abomination," "a devil," and "a thing." They had tried unsuccessfully to destroy him on more than one occasion.

But in his heart, he believed he was a man. No, he knew he was a man, despite what others said to the contrary. Yes, perhaps he was a different sort of man, unique compared to any that had come before him, but still a man. He felt his father had slighted him greatly, and as such, he had chosen to give himself a name.

He recalled the day his father had been screaming obscenities at him and referring to him as something which the bowels of hell spit upon the earth. In one of his first fits of anger, Adam had risen in defiance and had shouted at his father, "I ought to be thy Adam!"

He decided right then to take the name Adam. And in further rebellion against his heartless father Victor, he chose to use his father's surname. He proclaimed himself Adam Frankenstein. He hoped that single act would do more to frustrate his creator than any other torture he might have imagined. And he was correct. Since then, the story of his creation had gained legendary status; most people now referred to him simply as Frankenstein. Despite his life of solitude, his knowing this fact seemed to make it all worthwhile somehow. His father had died in disgrace, and the world that had shunned Adam was now essentially dead as well.

Since the time he had last escaped persecution, he had led a life of isolation, knowing how people would react to the sight of him. If his height and massive size were not enough to instill terror, his thousands of scars from where his doctor/father had stitched together body parts were enough to horrify even the most tattooed and pierced of humans. Through the centuries, people around the world had claimed to see him lurking in the shadows. However, anyone who had the misfortune of actually meeting him face to face would take that knowledge to the grave with them. Adam was not happy about killing humans, but on occasion, it was something he had to do and which he had reluctantly accepted.

Even in 2053, in a world ravaged by a zombie apocalypse where rotting remnants of humanity still feasted on the flesh of the living, he knew he would be considered a horrible monster. He read rumors stating that the Z43 virus was mutating in living outlander humans during the past year. Rather than waiting until death to activate, the virus was causing living humans to mutate into an assortment of strange inhuman creatures, some of which supposedly were as big as he was.

Perhaps in another few decades, things would change. Maybe the virus would continue to mutate, creating a new race of creatures so disturbing in appearance that Adam would not seem so frightening. Until then, he had his cave, his literature, and an unquenchable thirst for knowledge to keep him occupied.